Goddess Gilded in Gold

Taken and punished by My Girlfriend's Stepmother

By Julia S. Rose

Copyright © All Rights Reserved

ISBN: 9798602428421

Contents

Chapter One

When Judi and I started dating she insisted I meet her stepmother. Having only been to bed with Judi a few times I thought it was rather premature but after her constant insistence I decided it may not be a bad idea to please Judi and get some points in. I thought maybe Judi was actually serious about having a relationship with me. Being five years older than me I was sure she was looking for some kind of lasting relationship. Neither of us were virgins but I could tell by the way Judi acted in bed she was a lot more experienced than I especially with her insistence with me to please her orally whenever we made love. I was quite inexperienced at cunnilinigus having licked pussy only to seduce my girlfriend into sucking my cock but I never really give her an orgasm with my mouth rather I insisted on using my cock instead. With Judi things were different; her pussy was closed for business until I learned how to make love to her with my tongue insisting on having an oral orgasm first before intercourse. I spent hours under the sheet servicing her pussy with my tongue lying on my belly rubbing my erection uselessly between the sheet and my own belly trying desperately for some kind of relief. When she finally allowed me to screw her pussy Judi made the point that if I didn't make her orgasm with my cock she insisted on me going down on her licking up the mess and giving her an oral orgasm. I learn right away who was in charge and that my own pleasures were second to Judi's.

Judi's stepmother lived by herself in very exclusive 5 bedroom 3 bath home with a backyard private Roman bath in a tropical setting. We drove up to the house in my red VW and I was almost embarrassed when I saw that she had a new Mercedes parked outside in the driveway. Judi told me not to worry grabbing my hand walking me up to the door. Judi promised that her stepmother wouldn't bite yet guaranteeing that if she liked me I would get more than I ever imagined. She had already warned me that the pool area was for nude swimming only and that since today was scorching we would probably be invited for a swim.

The door opened up and to my surprise a rather large 5ft. 9in. tall buxom rather short haired brunette butch looking woman wearing only a black diaphanous robe and heels wearing a big smile on her face welcomed us to come in. I couldn't take my eyes off her large breasts because her nipples were pierced with sparkling gold rings. Judi introduced her stepmother as Jackie and then introduced me. To my surprise Jackie pulled my face into her large bosom giving me a warm hug thanking me for enjoying her pierced nipples. Grabbing me by my ponytail pulling my mouth to hers she gave me an open mouth kiss for a full minute licking my lips as she kissed. I actually enjoyed getting kissed by her and sensing this she slammed the front door shut with her foot grabbed the back of my head pulling my mouth back into hers forcefully kissing me thrusting her tongue into my mouth tickling my palate with the very tip of her talented tongue. Finally breaking the kiss leaving me quite sexually shaken Jackie complemented Judi on finding a guy with such supple kissable lips.

I was out of breath and red face embarrassed but I had nothing to say being so shaken other than I was very pleased to meet Jackie as both women started giggling. Jackie looking me in the eyes telling me I wouldn't be a problem getting along in this family by the way I allowed her to kiss me like that making me blush again. I gave Judi a look of disbelief but she just winked at me and told me to zip it. Jackie put her arm around me saying that she was going to be able to teach me allot about getting along with women. Giving me a swift swat on the ass Jackie complemented me on my spankable cheeks promisingly she was going to test me out later. I gave Judi another look and she was just giving me a nasty smile. Judi already warned me that her stepmother was a strict dominant type believing in physical punishment and goddess worship. Judi told me that even though she is 25 years of age her stepmother still disciplines her whenever needed. Judi also warned me not to be surprised if she pulls me over her lap for a spanking. After that hard swat on the ass I knew that sometime tonight I was going to get a spanking from her and it actually sounded exciting.

Jackie asked me if I liked soaking in a Jacuzzi. Before I could answer she just took both of us by the hand leading us outdoors to the beautiful Roman bath. There was an outdoor Jacuzzi, showers, and a large pool with a diving board surrounded by beautiful tropical flowers. Slipping off her see through robe Jackie stripped naked before us. The first thing I noticed was that her nipples were pierced with glistening gold rings with diamonds hanging from each one. I couldn't help looking down noticing Jackie's shaved pussy seeing a sparkle where her clitoral hood was pierced with a matching ring and diamond just like her nipples. Even though Jackie looked like she was slightly above average weight she had the looks of a 40 year old goddess with a curvy body that was getting me rock hard.

This was a first for me having never met a girlfriend's mother who stripped completely naked minutes after we kissed. Judi started stripping and Jackie grabbed my belt and started to unfasten it as soon as it was loose she unzipped my pants pushing my pants and shorts to my knees. Before I knew it Jackie had me completely naked and was busy fondling my genitals complementing me on my size. Although she mentioned I needed some pubic hair trimming with a few good squeezes she stroked me completely hard. Looking at Jackie's crotch I saw that her labia lips were quite enlarged just like her daughter Judi which Judi explained to me this was from a process of stretching during oral sex. I'm learning how to do this to Judi as well.

Seriously looking into Judi's eyes still squeezing my erection

Jackie told Judi that there's no way she's going to pass up sitting on my cock telling Judi she's just going to have to share tonight. Giving me a wink Judi told Jackie she could have all the cock she wanted and fucking me wouldn't bother her in the least.

I could see Jackie's labia lips were stretched bigger than Judi's who actually confessed to me that both their enlarged labia's were from their obsession with oral sex. Judi actually sat on my face and gave me instructions on how to pull her labia lips with my mouth helping them to stretch even farther every time we have oral sex. Judi wanted to get her labia pierced with golden rings enabling her to lace them together with a beautiful gold chain. Touching her pinky fingernail at my pee hole Jackie told Judi it would be nice to get my cock pierced telling her it would look so good with a nice big gold rink in my pee hole to lead me around with. My face turned red with embarrassment from the thought of a needle pushing into my most delicate flesh. Noticing I was getting a little squeamish Jackie let go of my cock changing the subject.

Grabbing me by my cock and grabbing Judi by worming Jackie's middle finger into Judi's ass Jackie led us to the large outdoor shower which automatically turned on as soon as we stopped under the showerhead. Both women started soaping me up using their breasts to wash my chest and back and their fingers to massage my cock and balls taking turns goosing my asshole. I notice both Judi and Jackie used their left hand for the asshole and the right hand to wash each other's pussies as well as my cock and balls. With Jackie masturbating my cock with her soapy hand I was rock hard once again. She rhythmically massaged my cock. I could barely stand up from all the pleasure Jackie was giving me. When I looked down Judi was doing the very same thing to Jackie fingering her butthole and pussy at the same time. With all this nastiness going on I knew I wasn't going to get out of here without getting spanked and fucked by her.

The girls finally stopped all the finger fucking, washed their hands off, and started kissing each other. This was more than just a mother daughter kiss on the cheek it was a full girl on girl tongue exchange that lasted for several minutes. I've never seen two women kiss before let alone a stepmother/daughter team. By the way they were kissing it seemed like they have been doing this for a long time because looked so natural as they enjoyed exploring each other's mouths. I found out later Jackie was fishing for the taste of my come in Judi's mouth to see if she had sucked me off.

Instead of feeding my ego allowing me to continue being a voyeur Jackie forced me to my knees opened her legs grabbed my ponytail pushing my head into her crotch ordering me to start licking. Both Judi and Jackie started kissing passionately as I pushed my tongue into Jackie's pussy. I could tell Jackie liked her pussy eaten similarly to Judi because when I started tongue fucking her Jackie pushed even harder around the back of my head telling me to thrust deeper with my tongue. Judi kneeling next to me tapped me on the shoulder wanting her turn. I couldn't believe it I was watching my girlfriend eating her stepmother's pussy with a passion. I actually got on the ground and was able to push my tongue into Judi's pussy. We stayed in this position for several minutes as the warm water continued spraying our bodies. My own cock was rock hard just from eating pussy. I think the taste of pussy juices for me is a perfect aphrodisiac keeping me hard as long as I'm licking. I could hear Jackie ordering Judi to start licking her clit. I found out later on that just by flicking her clit ring this stimulated her orgasm just like it was ringing a bell.

When Jackie started to come I was sucking on Judi's swollen clitoris at the same time and she started coming as well squirting juices into my mouth. I could see Jackie coming from above splashing Judi's face with juices and to my surprise she also started pissing giving both of us a golden shower in the shower. The warm water mixed with a spray of Jackie's golden fluids triggered Judi and to my surprise she began to squirt directly into my mouth forcing me to swallow some of it to keep from drowning. These nasty girls were willing to introduce me to every kinky fantasy I ever had. I always dreamed of drinking golden champagne and now I was swallowing Judi's orgasm stream just to keep from choking. Jackie was doing the same thing to Judi who was swallowing just as fast trying to keep up with the flow.

Jackie gave her daughter an open kiss on the mouth thanking her for the orgasm.

I was still eating Judi's pussy licking up the rest of her as Jackie looked down complementing me that her daughter has trained me well. Ordering me to lie on my back I stopped licking Judi and rolled over being obediently docile. Jackie straddled my waist grabbed my cock pointing it directly at her pussy telling me to let go. When I let go the stream was so intense it triggered another orgasm. Judi was so horny she sat back of my face facing Jackie placing her asshole right over my mouth to lick. She squealed as I pushed my tongue all the way up her anus. When I finished Jackie used the head of my cock to stimulate her clitoris as she continued coming in the throes of multiple orgasms started by her daughter's mouth. Judi was cursing calling me all kinds of nasty names as I cleaned her asshole like a bottle brush with my tongue. I was fortunate that her mother had finger fucked Judi quite deeply and it was only tasting a little soapy. Finally, realizing that Judi was having me service her asshole with my tongue Jackie slapped her right across the face because now my mouth was going to have to be washed thoroughly with soap if they were going to have me eating pussy tonight.

Pulling Judi off my mouth she took the pump soap from the shower ordering me to open my mouth and started squirting my tongue with disinfecting soap. Forcing me to gargle then spit it out she handed me a bottle of mouthwash making sure I gargled once again. Grabbing me by the balls squeezing hard she told me I was getting a little prematurely familiar with her daughter and eating her ass was a little too advanced for my lovemaking so maybe she was going to have to teach me a lesson as soon as we get out of the shower.

Jackie turned the water off from the shower telling both Judi and I things were getting quite nasty and had to stop. It was time for her to show her authority and establish some boundaries in this new relationship. Jackie asked Judi permission to give me a whipping. When Judi told her that would not be a problem Jackie said then I'm going to start with you first so that he will see what kind of a whipping I give. I think it would be appropriate out here in the garden to give you a nice intense caning. Right next to the shower was a flower pot with several inconspicuous canes sticking out of the dirt. Jackie reached for the thinnest one grabbing Judi leading her over to a marble bench adorned with four naked women holding it up as the feet. Jacky cursed pushing Judi over it butt up warning her to stay down and not move. Jackie also warned me not to touch my cock as she gave her stepdaughter a caning. Judi had a beautiful round ass that was as white as snow. As soon as Jackie started whipping her with lightning bolt strikes streaking her bare cheeks with full lines of welts from the top of her cheeks all the way down to her knees, by the time she finished her white ass was now crimson red with tiny shallow welts. Judi could hardly hold still during whipping which only took a minute leaving her quite shaken and in tears. Shaking the cane in my face seeing the scared look on my face Jackie promised she would get to me later giving Judi a hard swat on the butt telling her to get up or she would continue.

Chapter Two

Jackie suggested we all get into the Jacuzzi. Kissing each other on the mouth giving the girls a slippery taste of their pussy juices Jackie gave me another swat on the ass promising me she was going to give me a real sensual spanking as soon as she sampled my cock. Leading me by my stiff cock to the Jacuzzi Jackie had me step in and sit down and to my surprise she sat down facing me swallowing my cock with her pussy. Judi sat down next to us and started sensuously kissing me as Jackie started rising and falling on my cock pushing her large breasts into my chest. I couldn't believe that I was being charmed by my girlfriend and her stepmother in such a beautiful place. Fucking me ever so slowly to keep me from coming Jackie pulled free so that Judi could have a turn. Judi sat down keeping my cock buried in her pussy and just rotated her hips slowly to keep me hard kissing her mother at the same time. Every two minutes the girls traded places giving me a break in between squeezing my balls pulling them away from my body to keep me from prematurely shooting off.

After about ten minutes of fucking like this Jackie made me get out of the Jacuzzi and laying me on the cement on my back ready for more fucking. Jackie straddled my hips lowering herself back on my cock Judi facing her stepmother lowered herself on my mouth so that I could eat pussy and get fucked at the same time. Soon the women were French kissing enjoying using my body at the same time. Judi was wet and dilated accepting my tongue full depth in her vagina. Judi was busy fingering her clit as she rode my mouth.

I could feel Jackie squeezing me with her talented vaginal muscles which were so much like a mouth she took me over the top causing me to begin to squirt deep inside of her pussy. I could hear Jackie telling Judi that I was coming telling her to get off my face and get her mouth down to her crotch. It was something to watch when Jackie pulled my cock out of her pussy. Judi skillfully caught all of my sticky fluids on her tongue swallowing every last drop. Sucking on Jackie's clitoris it didn't take long and Jackie was squirting herself into Judi's mouth and all over her face. As soon as Jackie finished coming she started kissing and licking Judi sharing the fluids.

Looking at me with this "evil eye" look, Jackie grabbed me by the balls pulling me over her lap right there next to the Jacuzzi where the three of us just made love. Jackie told me she has a rule that any boy who violates her pussy must be punished. Since this was only my first time she was only going to give me a bare bottom bare handed spanking instead of using a more serious instrument like a strap or cane. Jackie said that she gave Judi a reprieve on a more severe whipping because of her fantastic mouth on her pussy and how creative an orgasm she gave her. As I lay helplessly over Jackie's lap she began massaging my cheeks complementing me on how spankable they're going to be and how much she is going to enjoy giving me my first spanking. Jackie was surprised how naïve and submissive I was automatically volunteering to get the spanking. Ordering Judi to go to cut her a fresh rattan cane (a bamboo) Jackie still wanted to give a demonstration of her abilities. Keeping me over her lap and massaging my cheeks she began fingering my asshole finding me quite comfortable to get penetrated by her middle finger.

As Jackie continued fingering my butthole Judi returned with tears in her eyes with a fresh cut rattan cane. I looked up at Jackie giggling telling Judi how much her new boyfriend enjoys having his butthole violated so she couldn't wait to take him into the bedroom and give me a real treat. Slipping her finger out of my asshole Jackie give me a slap across both cheeks ordering me to kneel down and watch my girlfriend get a real whipping. I found out that the first caning that Jackie gave Judi was only a warm-up and that Jackie prefers giving double whippings which are far more effective bringing the fear of the unknown. Kneeling at the end of the chair Jackie ordered Judi to get up on the bench on all fours with her head down and her bare bottom waving in the air for a perfect target. Placing the cane in her right hand Jackie stepped behind and to the left side of Judi swishing the cane through the air making sure she had the right distance. Stepping back a little she then asked Judi to hold still for volleys of three licks promising 37 stripes before she finished. Judi's ass was still red I couldn't believe she was about to get another caning.

With a stern look on her face Jackie reminded Judi to hold still during the switching but afterwards she will allow Judi to scream, curse, and wiggle all she wants. She must properly present herself once again for the next set of stripes. Turning around and looking at her stepmother in the eyes Judi weakly shook her head a "yes". Jackie replying in a gruff voice told Judi that she loved her but unfortunately she was going to have to suffer the stripes. Looking at me Jackie solemnly explained their values are based on worshiping the goddess, obeying the certain Commandments, and bowing down to the

Mistress of the house who has the final word who administers all punishments. Jackie reminded me that both her daughter and I violated her sacred trust forming a sexual union without her consent. According to the karmic law Judi must pay otherwise she may receive a fate seven times worse. Jackie told me that even though she knows that Judi seduced me I'm guilty just by participating in the act. For me I will suffer punishment in the privacy.

Grabbing Judi by the hair and raising her head off the cushion so that she could look her directly in her eyes Jackie asked her if she understood the reason why she was going to receive the more severe caning. I could already here Judi weeping as she told her stepmom she was guilty and voluntarily agreed to be caned. Jackie bent over giving her a long kiss on the mouth. When she broke the kiss she told Judi that she was sorry but was only carrying out the law of her household as representative of the goddess. Judi nodded saying that she understood telling her not to hold back the switch. Jackie told her that's not an option telling her stepdaughter she was deserving of the full brunt of the cane.

Jackie raised the cane high in the air allowing it to strike the top of Judi's bare cheeks which looked like it disappeared into Judi's flesh as the cane finally bouncing out leaving a thick red line across both cheeks more pronounced than the first one. Snapping the cane three times in one second leaving three distinct mark's Judi let out a chilling scream louder than when she got the stripes that were already burning on her bare striped ass. Allowing Judi to rest and properly present her ass she wiggled around for fifteen seconds settled down and pushed her ass high in the air for more. Jackie struck again leaving three more stripes below the others. Again Judi let out a howl as more tears streamed down her face. Jackie reminded Judi the reason she was getting a second caning was so Jackie could show off for her new boyfriend and take me to bed afterwards. Judi's cries made my own heart begin to race reminding me that my time to be disciplined was next. This time Jackie caned Judi more slowly taking around ten minutes using the same three lick cadence throughout the whipping leaving her cheeks black and blue and streaked with deep red welts this time. Admiring her handiwork Jackie began teasing and pinching each welt making Judi jump and wiggle all over being constantly reminded of each and every delivered deserving blow.

Pulling Judi to her feet Jackie drew her head into her bosom pushing a nipple into her mouth and stroking Judi's hair. The whipping reduced her into a child again as she slowly suckled on the nipple. Talking softly to Judi Jackie commended her on how well she took the caning and that according to the laws of the goddess her sinful ways are now forgiven. Jackie promised that tomorrow the three of us will surely celebrate.

Leaving Judi to herself Jackie pointed the cane directly in my face wishing she had known me for least another month because this was the only time she was going to have mercy on me and not blister my ass with the same cane as well. She called the housemaid on the intercom to come and get Judi to bed. The housemaid was a beautiful Jamaican woman named Myra who quickly walked up to the three of us completely naked. Her beautiful black flesh glistened in the sun and she gave Jackie a rather lustful smile. Jackie introduced Myra to me telling her that I was Judi's new boyfriend but would be spending the night with her in bed. Myra held out her hand and I gently took it kissing her fingers. Jackie told me she was impressed by such an appropriate gesture since Myra is superior to me being a Magical priestess. Jackie told Myra she was to take Judi off to the guest room and attend to her welts giving her the freedom to spend the night with her. Jackie also asked Myra to bring wine into her bedroom for us.

Chapter Three

Myra lead Judi away still sobbing from the painful whipping. I could see Myra stop and snake her middle finger into Judi's butthole fingering it deeply as they walked away. Jackie giggled telling me that Myra was quite skilled with a strapon so Judi was going to get quite a workout in all of her orifices tonight. Leading me away to her Mistress bedroom Jackie nastily pushed her middle finger into my butthole telling me I was going to get the same treatment as Judi. I started to sweat because I had read about strapon sex before and had seen pictures in magazines of women fucking guys but the studs never seemed to be enjoying it. Would I agree to it? There were also the homophobic feelings being violated like that I have to deal with something that I never really thought about before until now. Jackie told me that she knew by the way my asshole puckered when she mentioned strapon penetration that I had a lot of fear but reassured me that once we entered her boudoir I would come out the next day a completely changed person.

Forcing me to my knees making the crawl into the room Jackie grabbed me by my ponytail leading me through the sliding glass door into the Mistress bedroom. I couldn't believe how big of a room it was. The bed of was a round big enough for six people with red diaphanous draperies all the way around closing it in for privacy. The lighting over the bed was filtered red making it quite a sensuous place for lovemaking. I noticed several video cameras over the bed which could easily record everything that went on. Next to the bed was a large vanity with a beautiful mirror so Mistress could sit down and apply her expensive makeup. There was a flat screen TV on the opposite wall that was already showing some very explicit lesbian play. The room was filled with various tables, footstools, and elegant leather lounge chairs perfect for making love in every imaginable position. I could see marble statues around the room of woman performing intimate lesbian lovemaking techniques to each other. My favorite one was of two women in the 69 position that was made into a coffee table by placing a large round plate glass over the top woman. Next to the bed was a large stature of a completely naked goddess Diana with her legs opened wide beckoning someone to enjoy her pussy. The skilled stone mason actually made her pussy so that it was slightly dilated and was open for someone's tongue. There was also a statue of King Neptune holding his pitchfork with a huge 10 in. erection. There was a spray bottle and a box of wipes next the statue so I was sure that Neptune has had plenty of company.

Jackie led me over to the statue of Diana pushing me flat on my belly before her. Reverently she went over to the statue kneeling down and kissing the goddess' pussy. Calling me over she urged me to do the same thing. I slowly stuck my tongue into the goddess pussy slightly licking and kissing just like Jackie did. Jackie told me she was sure I pleased the goddess because tonight you're going to serve the goddess in every imaginable way. Grabbing me by the ponytail she led me to the bath which was right behind the bed through a hidden inconspicuous door. The entire bathroom was made of white marble. There was a bidet, a toilet and three marble sinks with gold faucets. Behind the sinks the entire wall was mirrored. In the corner of the room was a large open shower with several shower heads. There was also a sunken bathtub which four to six people could easily get inside.

After watching Judi take such a whipping I knew I could expect just about anything from Jackie.

Grabbing me by the ponytail pushing her pussy into my mouth she started squirting pee into my mouth forcing me to gulp it down. Rubbing my face talking dirty to me she continued feeding me until her bladder was empty forcing me to continue licking and cleaning her precious goddess cup. Slapping me across the face she told me never be embarrassed about anything we do together.

Pulling me off the toilet Jackie yanked me into the shower scrubbing my entire body like a German nurse with soap and water. Spending most of her time on my butthole Jackie using her two middle fingers of her right hand to get me to relax began pulling my anus open as a jet of water trailed from her fingers into my hole. Finger fucking me with a mild soap she kept the water moving in and out of my ass. Slapping me several times on the ass cursing that I was all to free by allowing my asshole to be touched in such an intimate way without objection Jackie told me she actually started doubting my virginity. Forcing me to kneel she slapped my face back and forth several times telling me to admit to having anal sex. Looking up into her eyes I honestly told her that the only anal penetration I had during my life was from an enema denying any other kind of penetration from another woman or a stud. Finally Jackie believed in my honesty she gave me another hard slap across the face telling me before she took my virginity it was time to face the music and suffer the same fate her stepdaughter Judi did.

Jackie told me she loves the sound of someone getting spanked in this bathroom so this will be the perfect place to give me my punishment. Taking some cord from the drawer she quickly tied me by the wrists to a towel rack ensuring there would be no escape from her wrath. To my surprise Jackie produced an 18 in long rubber strap that had a wooden handle. Grabbing me by the balls pushing the rubber strap into my face she ordered me to take a good look at it than forcing me to kiss it as an acceptance to her discipline. Telling me I could freely shout out. Jacking sternly told me that the only thing I can start begging for is forgiveness. Sprinkling water all over my bare ass the whipping began. I couldn't believe how much the strap was stinging my bare cheeks as Jackie stood behind me rapidly smacking me all over. She even whipped my thighs and calves causing me to almost fall over. On about the tenth spank I began cursing and after the first few minutes I started begging her forgiveness. The rubber strap was light and made a loud noise when it struck my bare flesh but its main value was to produce fear in the spankee. I surly was afraid and shaken from the mild strapping. Stopping momentarily she grabbed my hair yanking my head back kissing me fully on the mouth sucking my tongue out and softy biting the tip. She thanked me for begging forgiveness because I finally admitted to being guilty.

Dropping the rubber strap Jackie reached for a wooden paddle instead which would cause a lot more pain. Jackie promised to beat my sinful nature into submission and resumed the paddling. The oak wood paddle was 4ins. and wide and 18ins. long large enough to cover both of my cheeks at once causing me to cry out after every resounding blow. The sound of the paddle resonated off the floor, walls, and ceilings making it sound ten times louder than it actually was scaring the daylights out of me. It seemed like my bare cheeks were continuously on fire. When I looked around I could see Jackie smacking my ass with both hands on the paddle like a baseball bat with an intense look on her face. I lost count of how many spanks she gave me after 20 but by the time she finished I know it was over 30 blows. My cheeks were throbbing and I was once again begging forgiveness. Jackie grabbed me by the ponytail once again yanking my head back telling me that forgiveness has a price and that I have not paid it yet.

This time Jackie produced a short flogging whip with 11 tails of thin spaghetti like rubber that Jackie called a "stinger" and started whipping my back with flicks of her wrist making me jump all over from it sting. I had never been struck by a flogger and it didn't take long for me to respect this whip. Making sure she covered every last square inch my back and shoulders I was beginning to think I would've been better off getting the caning. After a couple minute flogging Jackie seemed bored. To my surprise she slipped a cane out of the Chinese vase in the bathroom. Complimenting me on how well I took the whipping Jackie decided to give me her trademark crisscrossing caning administering thirteen stripes on my bare ass. Warning me that it will be a lot less painful if I relaxed my cheeks, Jackie promised she will not do the switching with full intensity like she did her daughter. With that reassurance as soon as she saw my muscles relax she began the caning crisscrossing my cheeks with thirteen licks in less than ten seconds. I had never been caned before so even though she promised not to use a full swing the switch still stung and frightened me to tears. I was screaming out still moving around as if I was still getting caned a full minute after she administered the final blow.

Dragging me off to bed Jackie told me the only way I was going to finally please the goddess was for her to take my anal cherry. Jackie explained that at twenty years old I was the perfect age ripe for it. Pushing me into her huge bed I watched Jackie slowly strapon a black leather studded harness. Showing me several dildos she promised me that within a year I will be begging for more. Picking up a 9in. long dildo that was only 1- 3/4in. in diameter Jackie had a big smile on her face promising me that this one is going to sear in my memory the time she took my virginity with it. Pushing the flesh toned dildo into the ring over her crotch it still looked quite intimidating. Kneeling before me Jackie grabbed me forcing my head down ordering me suck the dildo.

When I started sucking the head Jackie pushed the back of my head forcing the dildo down my throat causing me to choke and gag drooling all over the dildo. Giving me a few more deep thrusts she pulled the dildo out of my slobbering mouth finally admitting that I'd definitely had no cock sucking experience. Forcing my head back down she told me to continue sucking the dildo and start contemplating having her cock sliding in and out of my asshole. I could feel her goosing me with lubricant something. Pulling the dildo back out of my mouth Jackie wanted me to verbally give her permission to take my cherry.

First I told her that I respected all of her beliefs apologizing for having sex with Judi without asking. I told her of getting whatever the goddess has declared in order make amends for my wrongdoing. I told Jackie that we've already made love several times and I've tasted her golden champagne I would be fine wuth her to take my anal cherry. I told her I have some homophobic fears that once I'm taken I will be thirsting for hard cocks instead of women. After coming across videos and reading about strapon sex in adult magazines I had always imagined being taken by an older but sexy dominant woman who was skilled telling Jackie I was definitely attracted to her.

Thanking me for the compliment Jackie told me that there was no one who is more skilled than herself to take my cherry. Being a queen goddess she has certain bragging rights telling me she has taken more cherries from the college girls and boys that she can count. Jackie told me that the girls are more squealers than the boys when getting fucked in the ass adding that most the boys actually enjoyed getting fucked after the first minutes. Jackie told me she has a feeling I'm something special so she is going to take me nice and slow in several different positions. Jackie giggled giving me a kiss on the lips telling me she has all day and night long to fuck my tight asshole into submission giving me a pat on the butt adding by the time she is done with me I will be begging for it.

Chapter Four

Placing a pile of pillows in the center of the bed Jackie gave them a pat inviting me to lie face down. As soon as I was in place Jackie gave me a hard smack on the butt reminding me that all I had to do was hold still, obey every word she tells me. Moving around in front of me Jackie started waving her cock in my face finally rubbing my lips with the large head. Jackie then started giving me a serious talk about the fear of homosexuality. Telling me what she believed that the goddess religion taught her was that pleasure for both men and women sometimes come together. As long as someone is not coerced, forced, or even raped then both men and women can satisfy each other's sexual urges freely.

Once my asshole has been stretched and trained I will have no trouble accommodating any of her male friends. She was even assured me that once I got over the fear I would be fucking men in the ass as well and making them suck my cock after I came inside of them. Jackie reminded me of the whipping she just gave her daughter would be worse for disobedience which will be a good incentive for me to experiment.

Telling me to purse my lips as if they were my anus she proceeded to attempt penetrating of my mouth. Instructing me on the working parts of my anus Jackie reminded me of my sphincter muscle which must be penetrated which can be quite painful at the very beginning. As I fought she pushed the head of the dildo into my mouth telling me that my lips were a little bit like my sphincter muscle suggesting that if I concentrated on relaxing it would not be as painful. The same thing holds if you relax your mouth and throat. To my surprise as soon as I began to relax Jackie began pushing her dildo all the way down my throat until the ring on her harness was actually touching my lips. Telling me to concentrate on holding my breath she kept the dildo buried in my mouth for 30 seconds and then slowly pulled out. Taking a few deep breaths Jackie pushed the dildo back down my throat cutting off my air once again for another 30 seconds stroking my hair telling me in a soft voice to relax. Patting me on the head she told me that when she enters my asshole I'm going to have to do the same thing if she is going to bury her cock deep inside of me. Giggling she told me that the good thing is I will be able to curse, swear, and take deep breaths all the while she's fucking me.

Moving behind me Jackie grabbed my knees pulling my legs apart. Taking my sore whipped cheeks she pulled them apart and started licking her way from the top of my crack to my butthole. I could feel her skilled tongue swirling around and around tickling and massaging moving closer and closer to my asshole. When she reached my anus there was no hesitation and she began licking the sensitive areas around it making me squirm. I was quite nervous because all I could think about was her huge dildo penetrating me. I could feel her pushing her tongue inside fucking my hole as if it were a cock. I began moaning loudly each time she pushed her tongue inside. I didn't even know what the sexual act was called even though I had just eaten her daughter's asshole which she was punished for. I found out later that this intimate act is called "analictus" something I was going to become very accustomed to servicing Jackie's friends. Giving me a reach around Jackie's started stroking my cock as her tongue continued fucking my anus. I couldn't believe how much pleasure she was giving me especially after the whipping I just received. Surely taking a few licks for my wrongdoing was magical as Jackie exonerated me for my evil ways.

Pulling her tongue out of my rear Jackie sounded out of breath telling me that now was the time. Kneeling behind me Jackie gave my ass a slap giggling telling me her favorite thing to do is deflowering young boys with her strapon but today was going to be extra special since I was her daughter's boyfriend. Jackie told me to hold still and get ready for the ride of my life. Rubbing the head of the dildo up and down Jackie could tell I was a little tense so she began talking to me in her soft sexy seductive voice convince me to relax my anal muscles permitting her to enter me with the head of her cock. The whole time she was talking Jackie was delicately wiggling the head around and around my anus telling me to push as if I was expelling something. As soon as I started pushing this enabled her to push the head of the dildo inside my anus past my delicate unstretched sphincter muscle giving me the surprise of my life as I was filled with a burning pain followed by the immediate desire to expel the dildo. Listening to my heavy breathing knowing that I was a little tense Jackie promised me that that it already was too late to pull out so I may as well relax and give in for the pleasure.

Telling me to grab my cock with my right hand and start stroking which will help keep my mind off my asshole warning me not to come too soon because her cock never goes soft. I could feel Jackie slowly rotating the dildo like a drill forcing the head in deeper. I actually started getting pleasure when they head pressed against my prostate gland causing my cock to begin expelling. With the dildo inside at least 3in. Jackie skillfully started pushing and pulling the head of the dildo back and forth across my prostate gland making me begin to squirm as this new form of pleasure started rising up within me. I started stroking my cock in rhythm with the dildo forgetting all about the painful anal entry.

Jackie kept on urging me to keep stroking my cock talking to me in her sexy voice to stay relaxed so that she can finish deflowering me. I finally got the message and I continued straining which relaxed my anal muscles just enough for her to keep pushing. When she had the dildo 5in. inside Jackie started fucking me a little faster and harder forcibly inching the dildo farther and farther into me. I could feel the outside of my anus getting stretched to the max as my loose skin of my outer anus was pushed and pulled along her shaft. I was sure she loved the site of watching her dildo taking my cherry.

Stopping momentarily with the dildo still at the 5in. mark Jackie leaned forward stuck her long nails into my shoulders and told me to take a deep breath and then release. I could feel her beginning to rotate her hips and as soon as I expelled the air from my lungs Jackie lunged her powerful hips forward driving the dildo all the way inside to the hilt. I could even feel the cold brass ring against my anus. My entire body felt like it was on impaled on a fence post. My entire being wanted to buck Jackie off of me and work lose of her dildo. Keeping her hips tightly fastened against me Jackie held on to my shoulders riding me like a stallion. Every part of my psychological being told me I was on the wrong end of the stick. The stallion was supposed to be doing all the fucking. As I fought the losing battle all my homophobic thoughts came to mind. Bargaining with myself I admitted I was in the privacy of Jackie's bedroom getting taken by my freaking girlfriend's exotic stepmother and her artificial silicone cock. All she was sharing with me was to give me to understand of an alternative lifestyle that included a different way to view the world including a different kind of pleasure. I was also a captive in a mistress bedroom under her magical spells under her will. To Jackie pleasing the goddess seemed to mean subjugating men under her. Thinking like this comforted me some but I was still uncertain.

As soon as I stopped fighting and settled down taking a deep breaths and slowly gasping for air I turned around and admitted to Jackie it was too late she had taken my virginity and I wanted her to fuck me. Settling into the pillows I put my head down and arched my bottom upwards giving her better access to my asshole. Grinding the dildo around and around inside of me Jackie swatted my cheeks crying out loud glorifying the goddess that another boy has lost his virginity. Leaning forward Jackie recited a short prayer dedicating me to the goddess.

(I give you this boy who has willfully allowed me to take his virginity honoring the goddess. Free him from his homophobic fears and open up his

anus to new pleasures that I'm about to give him. My dildo which has opened up his asshole opened the door for me to give him male partners who also worship the goddess openly experimenting with his new sexuality. May he free from disease and only healthy partners couple with him. Free him from any fears of oral copulation as I teach him. I take charge of all of his sexual teachings making sure that he is taught methods he never knew possible and properly disciplined in obedience to the laws of the goddess.)

With the dildo slowly pulling out of my asshole I contemplated that she dedicated me to the goddess but I told myself that I just had to trust Jackie and new sexual possibilities will come to pass. Talking to me in her sexy voice Jackie told me to keep my legs open, relax and just enjoy the ride. I couldn't believe how good she used her hips twisting and grinding the dildo in and out plunging in full depth each time. My entire body rocked back and forth to the fucking. Instead of crying out like I did at first I started moaning joyfully concentrating on the head of the dildo sliding back and forth across my prostate. My cock was rock hard and spewing fluids each time she pressed forward. For the first time in my life I realized that getting fucked by someone with a cock I really didn't have to do any work but just enjoy my goddess treating me to anal intercourse. Soon Jackie had me by my hair pulling my head backwards and fucking me at the same time enjoying another boy she has successfully violated. I found out later on that Jackie had a wooden dildo with notches for every boy and girl she has stripped of their cherries.

Sliding the dildo faster and faster Jackie was getting quite turned on when I heard her passionate cries I started masturbating faster and actually came as she screamed in passion I started squirting my sperm wastefully all over my chest giving myself a sperm shower. I remembered Jackie telling me that her cock never goes soft like mine which was already going limp after spewing my come all over myself. I then realized that Jackie was multiorgasmic and definitely was not going to stop with her first orgasm of the night. I could tell my asshole was a little sore so I started bargaining with Jackie asking her for break.

Slapping me harshly telling me never to question a dominant woman telling me to just shut up and keep stroking my cock forcibly pushing my head back down on the bed telling me to keep my butt up so she could slide in and out of my ass easier. Jackie continued thrusting deeply pounding her thighs against my backside turning both of us into a sweaty duo.

Grabbing my sticky half limp cock I started stroking again and to my surprise with the dildo constantly sliding in my asshole I was actually getting excited again. I got another surprise when I felt the dildo begin to vibrate. I looked around to ask Jackie what was happening and she started giggling knowing that I just felt the vibrator turn on. Giving me several more playful slaps on the ass which still made me jump she told me that the vibrator will help both of us on our next orgasm telling me to just shut my mouth and enjoy. The vibrations definitely took my mind off my painfully stretched anus sending shivers up my spine. I could even feel my balls beginning to vibrate which seemed to help me gain back my erection.

I started thinking about when I fucked Judi yesterday she complained about my premature ejaculation forcing me to go down on her because I couldn't continue screwing her to orgasm. I can still see her pussy full of my cum as I was going down on her. Now I was finding out firsthand the power of a strapon because Jackie could screw me all night long as long as she had the energy because her larger silicone cock would never go soft.

The vibrations we're finally getting to me and I became more relaxed accepting my place beneath my Mistress. I began moving with her instead of against her slowly rotating my hips rhythmically to her thrusts. Jackie even complemented me finally giving in to her and enjoying the moment telling me that this is what it is going to be like from here on out. My mind started going crazy because I really didn't understand what she just said. Sensing my confusion which made me tighten my grip with my anal muscles on the shaft of the dildo making it harder for Jackie to continue thrusting forcing her to push the dildo all the way into me to the hilt, Jackie slowly rotating her hips and began explaining. Grabbing my ponytail pulling my head back so that I could see her face talking to me in a stern voice Jackie told me that taking my virginity tonight is just the beginning of my training promising me she and her daughter Judi will be involved in every nasty new thing that will happen to me. I'm going to be introduced to sexual sensations I never thought of before. Finally telling me the most important thing is just to relax and enjoy this moment getting fucked by a beautiful experienced mistress.

Giving me several more stinging slaps Jackie told me to settle down and get comfortable because she was going to ride my ass all the way home. Pulling her artificial cock almost completely out

Jackie turned off the vibrator telling us it was time for more lube. I could feel Jackie spilling lubricant down my butt and all over the dildo sliding it in and out several times and she continued pouring the cold gooey substance making my sore asshole easier to continue the fucking. Sliding the dildo back inside my ass she turned vibrator back on. I started playing with my cock again which was almost fully erect. This time with all the negative feelings and pain removed I actually was beginning to enjoy getting fucked by this beautiful dominant woman. I started crying out her name exclaiming; "Oh Jackie, Jackie" over and over again. And then I started crying "oh god" and Jackie corrected me with a sharp slap telling me to cry out "Oh Goddess" instead because this is what losing my virginity was all about pleasing the goddess.

Suddenly as the end of the dildo contacted my stretched anus it started giving me a small electric shock making me internally jump a bit each time the dildo bottomed out. Giving me another slap on the ass Jackie started giggling telling me not to be shocked. Each shock was so intense it seemed to make sparks fly out the end of my cock causing it to become rock hard.

I found out later on that all of the nerve cells in my asshole and my cock are interconnected which was why the shocks were enabling my erection. I could hear Jackie squirming and crying out each time I was shocked telling me she was feeling the same thing through pussy lips. I told myself that this woman was one tough yet unusual lady actually enjoying the vibrations and shocks along with myself. All this extra stimulation sent me over the top first. Squeezing the head of my cock desperately trying not to come I felt Jackie's hand forcefully push mine away grabbing me by the balls pulling them away from my body just in time to save me from another premature ejaculation. Keeping her grip on my balls Jackie continued fucking, vibrating, and shocking me driving both of us to another powerful orgasm.

When Jackie started coming she pushed the dildo all the which made it give both of us a continuous shock. Releasing my balls I started coming into the palm of her hand ejaculating so much my semen I thought I completely emptied my balls.

Both of us were shaking from the vibrations and constant shock. Finally Jackie came down from her orgasm switching the dildo off. Pulling my head back Jackie took her handful of cum rubbing it all over my mouth forcing it open with her fingers and pushing all of it inside demanding that I swallow some. I gulped down another forced load as she treated me just like her stepdaughter. Telling me I was a good boy when she finally saw me swallowing. Jackie's own daughter Judi was the first one to indirectly make me to eat my own come right out of her pussy after fucking her but I was still not used to the thought of swallowing semen even if it was my own. It still seemed quite nasty an unnatural yet being forced to do something dirty was actually a turn on for me. Licking my lips free of come I told

Jackie that was the hottest orgasm I ever had. Jackie promised me she could do that for me all the time.

Jackie told me she was going to make a dildo change because now since my asshole was so relaxed I will be able to accommodate an even larger one. I watched Jackie walk over to her bureau where the housemaid had placed some wine pouring of us both a glass. My asshole was still tingling from the fucking and shocking but I obediently remained butt up over the pillows knowing I was about to be fucked once again. I was so overcome by lustful thoughts my hips were already moving as if I was getting fucked by a phantom cock. Watching me Jacking told me not to worry my body is now grieving for more cock which she will satisfy soon. She opened a drawer and pulled out a black 10in.long dildo that was at least 2in.wide in diameter. With a big smile on her face she slipped it into her harness stroking and pointing it directly at me telling me once I'm fucked by this cock Goddess Jackie will know she has finished the punishment.

Chapter Five

I was a little shaken from getting fucked twice already yet my asshole was twitching for more. I couldn't figure out why I was so sexually turned on. I found out later on that Jackie had slipped me something which helped me relax making me desire more sex along with the magic blue erection pill. Jackie brought me a glass of wine and sat down in front of me. As we sipped the expensive pinot noir wine Jackie told me I was the hottest boy she ever had the pleasure of taking and was definitely looking forward to fucking me again as soon as we finished our wine. Taking my hand and she placed it on her cock telling me to stroke it. As soon as I started rubbing the huge shaft I told her it was quite large. Jackie assured me that is surely was but with her in the saddle I had nothing to worry about. Finishing her glass of wine Jackie took my glass away from me setting it on a nearby table. Kneeling in front of me she started rubbing my cheeks with the head of the dildo telling me how much she enjoyed fucking me and how submissive I was at allowing her take me so easily. Jackie started telling me that this new dildo was crafted from her housemaid Myra boyfriend's cock confessing that she had the real thing pushed into own asshole just last week and maybe somehow that what happen to me. In a soft seductive voice she began rubbing my lips with the head of the dildo pulling my chin down telling me to open my mouth wide.

As soon as she had my mouth open she pushed the dildo inside a good 6ins. until I was gagging. Pulling back but keeping the dildo in my mouth she started giggling telling me now I know what it feels like for a man to force a huge cock into a woman's mouth undeservingly. Having already sucked and swallowed her smaller dildo this one was really going to be a challenge to swallow let alone taking it all the way into my asshole. The head of the dildo was definitely a lot larger than the last one which was going to take Jackie a lot longer to push it into my tight rear. I was actually getting turned on being forced face fucked with Jackie holding my ears pulling my mouth up and down the shaft with the head of the cock bouncing against my uvula. Fucking my face until my mouth had saliva drooling down my cheeks and chest until my throat was sore from forced cock sucking Jackie pulled the dildo from my mouth and started slapping my face back and forth with her cock until I saw stars telling me that even though she knew I didn't enjoy this experience there would be a lot more time for cock sucking in the future.

Taking a drink of my wine she handed the glass to me ordering me drink it all which

I quickly swallowed down. The wine actually had another "magic" potion which started making me horny again. I found out later on that Jackie was also taking a similar potion which helps ensure her to be multi-orgasmic all night long.

I could hear Jackie putting a rubber glove on her left hand and opening up a can of thick oily lube. With two greasy fingers Jackie started pushing them deep into my still dilated asshole massaging and stretching it until she got three fingers inside. Going slow and taking her time stretching and lubricating as she went Jackie was able to get all four fingers and part of her thumb stretching my anus to the max. I was already crying out to the goddess getting very uncomfortable and not knowing what was going to be next. Jackie kept reassuring me that she was in total control and would never let anything happen to my precious asshole because she has lots of plans for me. Jackie continued fingering me making sure that I was well lubricated. Finally she removed her fingers and snapped off the glove. I could feel the bulbous head of the dildo pushing against my anus like a large battering ram. Speaking softly to me ordering me to push just like I did for the other dildo with a little bit of straining she was able to get the huge head inside. As soon as the head popped past my sphincter muscle the sensation made me feel like I was getting ripped apart I started crying out and bucking once again.

Not wanting to cause pain Jackie pulled free and applied more lubricant to both my asshole and the huge black dildo. Wiggling the head Jackie pushed her battering ram back inside for another entry causing me to squeal like a baby. This time there was no mercy as I felt a steady pressure from Jackie's hips slowly driving the dildo inside. Rotating her hips like a drill using the same technique she used last time Jackie was able to get a good 7ins. inside quite fast. I could feel my insides spasming around the huge dildo and my anal muscles were clamping out of control trying desperately to expel the huge foreign object. Mistress was too skilled for this because she was determined to skewer me completely on all 10 inches. Ignoring my pleads for her to pull free, Jackie started fucking me nice and slow easing the dildo into me farther and farther every time she pushed inside. Slapping my butt real hard ordering me to stay relaxed and focus on pushing back it only took her some minutes and she had the entire dildo buried in my ass. Celebrating she began whipping my bare behind with both hands at the same time. She was spanking me so hard I was fucking myself by pulling away trying to get away from the spanking only to have her drive the dildo back inside with her powerful hips.

Squealing at the top of her lungs letting out a banshee cheer Jackie drove the dildo completely inside and started rotating her hips grinding away watching me squirm helplessly before her quite disturbed by the sudden impalement. This time my whole body was fighting the dildo as my entire being wanted to expel it immediately. Jackie started massaging my shoulders and back trying to get me to relax and she continued grinding away with the dildo forcibly pushing with her powerful hips keeping the huge shaft all the way inside of me. Pulling my head back by the ponytail which seemed to be her favorite thing to do Jackie told me to never forget this moment because I now have been taken by the queen goddess of strapons. Both of us should be proud of this moment. Jackie promised I was going to make a good cock sucking fuck-boy for her. Leaning forward reaching her hands all the way around my face sticking her middle fingers in the sides of my mouth like a makeshift harness pulling my head back Jackie started fucking me like she was riding a horse. I could feel her heavy breasts pounding on my back as her well developed hips drove the dildo in and out of my asshole. I felt totally taken melting beneath her submitting to every thrust of her cock.

Without even touching my own cock I started shooting another useless load of sperm all over the pillows beneath me. I totally felt like losing my manhood to this dominant woman who was fucking my ass taking me like a girl.

Mistress continued fucking me unmercifully working on her own orgasm. Screaming at me Jackie reveled in the fact that I already had another orgasm promising me that she had the energy to fuck me a lot longer than if I was fucking her so enjoy the ride. Letting loose of my mouth she dug her nails into my buttocks pulling them apart so that she could drive into me even farther pushing my body forward on every thrust.

Fucking me for another ten minutes causing me to go into a delirious trance-like

state; *(I actually went into a dream like state and met my lover Judi next to a beautiful waterfall. Both of us were naked getting turned on to our sexy bodies. We embraced and started kissing passionately falling to the ferns next to the water. My cock was rock hard knowing soon it would be thrusting in my lover. Finding me on my back as Judi continued kissing me I could feel her drawing my knees upward and outwards thinking that she was going to suck my cock. Suddenly I could feel the head of a hard cock pressing against my anus. I was confused and startled wondering how Judi had grown a cock. I could see her looking into my eyes with beautiful blue eyes almost hypnotizing me with a certain fascination telling me to use my own imagination and just accept what was happening. Talking to me in a soft seductive voice advising me to just give it to the sensations I could feel her cock slowly penetrating me. This time in the dream there was no pain but only pleasure. I felt the pressure of her cock sliding inside but the sensations overwhelmed me sending shivers of delight up and down my spine. It felt like Judi's fantasy cock kept sliding farther and farther inside of me taking over my entire being. Her huge cock began sliding in and out of my whole body. Contorting her body with her cock still fucking me Judi opened her mouth swallowing my cock completely. I could feel her tongue sliding up and down my shaft as her mouth sucked constantly beckoning my seed from my balls. I could feel her cock inside of me getting harder. It didn't take long and soon Judi was sucking the come from my cock swallowing every last drop. With her mouth continuing to suck my cock I could feel her own cock beginning to explode sending load after load of sticky juices into my body. Her nails turned into claws as she dug into my balls like a starving eagle. As she devoured my balls a new peace came over me and I accepted my new role. Withdrawing her cock from my well fucked asshole I looked down and where my cock was it was now a pussy. Smiling at me Judi had transformed into a hung stud complete with a huge cock and a full set of balls. My new pussy was wet so I opened my legs and welcomed her to fuck me. Walking into our dream Jackie came in wearing a strapon and holding a whip)*

Waking up from the trance screaming and crying I could feel Mistress still fucking me. I was actually happy to find that I still had a cock and balls yet I was getting fucked in the ass by the most beautiful mature woman I had seen. Crying out to the goddess Mistress finally had her final orgasm from fucking my devirginized ass for the night. This time after Jackie came the dildo slowly slipped from my asshole and I could feel copious amount of fluids dripping from my well fucked asshole. When I reached around and grabbed some of the fluids I recognize them as being semen. I knew the dildo that Jackie was using did not have a way to ejaculate yet there was copious amounts semen dripping from my ass. Crawling around in front of me Mistress knew that I was confused. She told me never to question her magic. The potion she had given me put me into a trance for an hour giving ample time for just about anything magical to happen. Someday I will tell you the truth but by then you will just laugh about it. I took a quick look between my legs at my cock making sure once again was still there. I felt like I just ejaculated and to my surprise my cock when smeared with lipstick all the way down to the base. When I looked up at Mistress her lipstick was also smeared and it was the same color that was on my cock. Her right cheek was still splattered with a squirt of fresh semen. I didn't say anything but I started to worry because this told me that she was sucking my cock while someone else was fucking me.

Holding the huge dildo with her right hand she grabbed the back of my head with her left hand and told me it was time to clean her strapon with my mouth. The huge dildo was covered with sticky foreign semen started making me sick to my stomach. Seeing my hesitation Jackie warned me that if I didn't clean it properly I would get the same caning that Judi got earlier. Teasing my mouth with the head of the dildo covered with come she began lubricating my lips with it forcefully pressing forward. Reluctantly I opened my mouth knowing where it has been and what has been inside of me I chose to please my beautiful goddess rather than take a caning. Sucking off the first 6in. of goo I swallowed without thinking knowing that Jackie wouldn't allow me to do anything that was going to cause me harm. I remembered that before the fucking she had been eating my asshole as well so if I was good enough for her it was good enough for me. Jackie guided my mouth forcing me to lick up and down the dildo until it was completely clean. Reaching around to my ass she caught a large gob of fluids in her hand, smiling at me she rubbed it all over my face slapping me across the cheek sending the fluids flying.

Pointing a finger at me Jackie told me she wanted me to know that my lover Judi watched every minute of our lovemaking on a live video screen in her bedroom. Explaining that they both know who violated me and Judi already messaged that it was hot watching me take it. Pulling me into her bosom Jackie gave me a long passionate kiss stroking my hair and congratulating me for being such a good boy welcoming me to the family. When she kissed me and pushed her tongue into my mouth I could taste my own come as I sucked her tongue. This definitely told me that goddess Jackie was capable of enticing me to do every nasty deed she desired even if I was in a dream state.

Knowing I was still thinking about what ever happened to me Jackie reassured me that she was in charge and it was her decision so I would just have to live with it because it's too late now. Jackie added that she was quite proud of me to be able to go this far this fast and after tonight she knew I was going to be able to accommodate anything whenever she demanded.

Leading me into the shower as the nice warm waters streamed over us Jackie gave me a slap on the ass telling that my homophobic fears are a thing of the past because she has plans for my asshole that I never thought of before. Jackie spent a lot of time cleaning her lipstick off my cock and balls unapologetic and never admitting she had given me a good sucking.

Chapter Six

As she toweled me off I started to cry as my emotions broke from all the nasty things I had done. Goddess Jackie held my head between her breasts stroking my hair and telling that I did nothing wrong because she was in charge and made all the calls. Jackie spoke in her calm seductive voice telling me I will feel better if I fall down and kneel before her for being such a naughty boy. Jackie knew exactly what I wanted. I fell to the floor kissing her feet. I started begging forgiveness for doubting the pleasures she introduced to me today. Jackie told me that I have pleased the goddess by asking forgiveness and she has the authority to forgive and to pronounce just punishment for any wrongdoings. Telling me to kneel before her and look into her eyes I quickly got up on my knees and looked into beautiful brown eyes. Once she saw me sincerely staring Jackie told me that once she pronounces judgment the punishment will immediately be carried out and afterwards I will be forgiven and we will never talk about it again asking me if that was clear? I could hardly blurt out the words but fearfully I told her I am ready to be judged by my goddess.

Escorting me back to bed Jackie treated me to long sensual massage. Oiling my body with her large breasts Jackie began massaging me. It was hot feeling her hard nipples rubbing against my bare flesh. Her fingers were busy manipulating every nook and cranny working out all the muscle knots and tensions from getting fucked and strapped. Jackie even oiled her labia lips rubbing them up and down my arms and legs finally giving herself an orgasm as she vigorously rubbed against my heel. Rolling me over on my back she continued rubbing her labia lips up and down my legs looking seductively into my eyes telling me how great of a body I had. She also commented unapologetically on what a spankable butt I had and how much she enjoyed punishing me telling me she was looking forward to many more memorable disciplinary moments in the future.

Working herself up my body with her tongue massaging my flesh she stopped to kiss and suck my nipples. Finally Jackie placed her luscious full lips over mine kissing me as we melted together. She spent a good minutes intensely kissing me getting me so hot I didn't realize that she slid her pussy over my cock swallowing it completely and slowly kneading me with her pussy muscles just to keep me hard. It was so sexually exciting to be fucked in different ways by a skilled dominatrix from above asserting her rightful place. I could feel her frigging her clitoris giving herself an orgasm pulling off my erection in time denying me one. Changing positions she straddled my face lowering her pussy on my mouth. Jackie instructed me to only lick her vagina pushing my tongue in and out deeply so when she felt me obediently tongue fucking her she bent forward and swallowed my cock. I couldn't believe that now I was 69ing with the queen goddess obediently under her where I belonged. I knew that only an hour earlier she had been sucking me yet her sexual appetite seemed unfulfilled as she voraciously sucked and licked my cock hard once again. When I felt her slowly pulling my tongue out of her pussy rubbing her pierced clitoris over my lips I knew she wanted it sucked.

Pursing my lips I took her clitoris into my mouth careful not to hurt her piercing and slowly began sucking. I could feel Jackie's lips wrap around the head of my cock as she began sucking and teasing my pee hole with the tip of her tongue. Both of us seemed to orgasm together. Jackie started Squirting fluids into my mouth and all over my face I could feel my body lunging upward as I started ejaculating into her mouth. All of my sexual glands at the same time were crying out trying to squeeze every last sperm cell into my goddess' mouth. I could feel six distinct squirts as my entire being came giving her my all. Sitting up swallowing Mistress raised her hands to the statues. Changing positions facing me so that her pussy was directly over my mouth I knew exactly what she wanted. After I finished washing her pussy with my tongue she thanked me giving me a warm loving kiss.

We fell asleep with me under the sheets with my head between Jackie's crotch.

Printed in Great Britain
by Amazon